# THE BLUE
# KYROLITE

ROBIN E. NEFT

**BALBOA.**
PRESS

A DIVISION OF HAY HOUSE

Balboa Press books may be ordered through booksellers or by contacting:

Balboa Press
A Division of Hay House
1663 Liberty Drive
Bloomington, IN 47403
www.balboapress.com
1 (877) 407-4847

Because of the dynamic nature of the Internet, any web addresses or links contained in this book may have changed since publication and may no longer be valid. The views expressed in this work are solely those of the author and do not necessarily reflect the views of the publisher, and the publisher hereby disclaims any responsibility for them.

The author of this book does not dispense medical advice or prescribe the use of any technique as a form of treatment for physical, emotional, or medical problems without the advice of a physician, either directly or indirectly. The intent of the author is only to offer information of a general nature to help you in your quest for emotional and spiritual well-being. In the event you use any of the information in this book for yourself, which is your constitutional right, the author and the publisher assume no responsibility for your actions.

Any people depicted in stock imagery provided by Thinkstock are models, and such images are being used for illustrative purposes only. Certain stock imagery © Thinkstock.

Print information available on the last page.

ISBN: 978-1-5043-3894-3 (sc)
ISBN: 978-1-5043-3895-0 (e)

Balboa Press rev. date:   03/10/2016

## CHAPTER 1

# FEARS

Scotty jumped. The stillness was shattered. Something scared him . . . again!

He was sitting behind a boulder out in the hot, dry, barren wastelands of Kestrellia, enjoying being alone, collecting the best, most awesome red crystals . . . until now.

Something had just blasted Scotty's peace and quiet into outer space. It was a weird, skidding, slithering sound. Something was moving around on the sand.

Then silence.

A moment and . . . there it was again.

Scotty imagined a snake slithering by . . . a poisonous snake, with gruesome green fangs.

Or maybe . . . maybe it was an evil alien or a bloodthirsty monster with three red glaring eyes, twelve arms and long sharp teeth.

Scotty was getting really scared, he could barely breathe. He was shaking. He could feel his cheeks getting hot while the palms of his hands sweated.

All Scotty ever wanted was to not be so scared of everything all the time.

Scotty had just arrived on Krestrellia a few days ago. He did not know much about this planet, this new world 350 light years from Earth. This was his first trip out to the arid, dusty, lonely, flat wastelands.

There was that sound again. Where was it coming from? "WHAT IS THAT?" he whispered, the sound of his own voice giving him only mild comfort.

Scotty did not expect to hear anything out here in the middle of nowhere, far from the earthbase where he lived with his dad and nanny. Nothing lived or grew here . . . or so he had been told. Scotty tried to count the minutes since he had heard the last sound.

Maybe it, whatever *it* was, was gone.

His imagination running wild, he waited. He was trying to breathe as quietly as possible. He was sure since his heart was pounding out of his chest it could be heard hundreds of miles away, to the very edge of the wastelands.

After a wait that seemed like forever he finally decided to brave it and climb to the top of the big boulder he had been sitting behind.

Then he changed his mind. Better to remain invisible. Make himself as small as possible. Curl up in a ball behind the boulder.

He was quivering behind the boulder, curled in a tight ball, shaking like a leaf, but trying not be heard, waiting and waiting and waiting.

Just then the most haunting melody filled the wastelands. The melody seemed to float on the air like the howl of a lone wolf. Scotty had never heard anything so beautiful. It echoed off the boulders scattered across the barren land, bouncing off the odd rock formations that popped up everywhere. But, where was the music coming from?

Scotty ever so slowly crept out from behind the boulder and gingerly climbed to the top of the big boulder. There, sitting on the ground on the other side of the boulder was a green-haired alien boy playing a beautiful, stringed instrument.

He was the strangest alien Scotty had ever seen: He had orange skin, blue antennae, purple eyes, and a button nose. The alien boy was wearing a loosely fitting silver shirt and pants. He had short, greenish-brown hair, a thin mouth, and tiny pointed ears. His skin shimmered in the sunlight from the planet's two suns.

Scotty hoped the alien had not spotted him. But before he knew it, the boy looked up and simply said, "Gavla". Hello.

Scotty, still trembling, replied, "G-ga-gavla."

"My name is Aldis, but everyone calls me Aldy."

"Wow, you speak English?"

"I speak perfect English. I learned it in school. What is your name?"

"Scotty. I just came to Kestrellia a few days ago. My dad is a scientist at the earthbase."

"So you will be living on Kestrellia now?"

"Not really. See, my parents are divorced. I missed my dad, so my mom said I could come visit him during my summer vacation."

"Well, great, at least you will be here for the summer. How old are you?"

"Nine."

"I am almost ten."

Why was I so scared? Scotty thought. This alien boy was really nice!

"Your dad is a scientist?"

"Yeah, he's the head of research at the earthbase. He's always working. I hardly ever get to see him."

"I am the son of . . ."

Aldy was the son of the planet's leader and it was best not to reveal this information to strangers. Kids might become his friends just because his dad was the king.

Before Aldy could even finish what he had been saying Scotty said, "I come out here when I want to think. Why are you out here?"

"I come out here when I want to write my songs and play my syth. It's noisy in my house. There are lots of people in there all the time. The wastelands are peaceful. I can stay out here all day and play music."

"That syth is pretty cool. I've never seen an instrument with rainbow colored strings. What are all the buttons for?"

"The different buttons are for unique sounds. I can make thousands of sounds with my syth. Do you want to learn how to play it?"

"Do I!"

The two boys spent the rest of the day filling the barren wastelands with beautiful music. Tired, hot, thirsty, and with the two suns of Kestrellia sinking, they decided to head for home.

"Hey Aldy, do you want to come back to my house for dinner?"

"Certainly. I have never been inside the earthbase."

"Great! I'll show you around a little bit."

Their boots kicking up dust all the way, the two boys walked the mile and half through the wastelands to where the earthbase was located on the small strip of land between the wastelands and mountains. There were a few trees, green plants and small streams in absolute contrast to the arid wastelands.

As they approached Scotty noticed that Aldy looked impressed.

"Scotty, what are those tall shiny purple spires in the middle of the base?"

"Those spires are the research buildings. They're made of a special metal: alurium. It lets you see out through the walls when you're inside, but you can't see into the buildings from the outside."

Aldy nodded.

"My dad works in the top floor of the highest spire. He's in charge of all research at the earthbase. Come on, let's ride the moving walkways."

The boys climbed the moving walkways that wound through the earthbase, connecting the spires and homes of the scientists. They passed by shops and several of the houses ringing the tall, purple spires.

"Scotty, are all those metal and glass buildings around the perimeter homes?"

"Yep and mine's the one right over there." Scotty pointed off to the left. "Let's go."

They hopped onto another walkway. As they approached the one-story glass and bronze-colored metal building, Zillian, Scotty's nanny, came running out, her long, flowing aqua hair trailing behind her. Her mouth was pulled tightly.

"Where have you been?" she yelled.

"Just hanging out with my new buddy, Aldy."

Zillian's deep gold-ringed, burgundy eyes grew wide. She gave Aldy a strange look.

For a minute Scotty thought Zillian recognized Aldy.

"I brought Aldy home for dinner."

"Well, okay, dinner'll be ready soon. You show Aldy around the house."

As they walked into the house Aldy appeared overwhelmed. "What is the floor made of? I love the way it sparkles under the lights in the ceiling."

"It's some kind of super-strong blue glass."

"And the pictures on the walls?"

"Those are 3D holograms of places on different planets that I visited with my dad and mom on vacations. If I stare at them long enough I almost feel like I could walk right into them and be on those other worlds again."

Aldy pointed to pictures on the other side of the room. "And what are these pictures of?"

"My uncle's farm in Old Iowa. That's where I'm from, Old Iowa. It was a state in an ancient country called the United States of America. We don't have countries anymore on Earth. We're one united planet like Kestrellia."

Zillian yelled from the kitchen, "Boys! Dinner is ready."

That night Zillian served a big dinner for the two boys, bigger than she had ever made for Scotty and his dad. It was a meal fit for a king. Scotty wondered why Zillian had gone to such trouble. Maybe it was because Aldy was the first friend he had ever brought home for dinner.

## Chapter 2

# ALIEN BUDDY

Several days went by before Scotty saw Aldy again. Scotty and his dad had gone hiking down by the streams that ran through the earthbase and found some cool green and gold mineral specimens. The next day Scotty's dad took him on a tour of the labs, he even got to help one of the scientists with an experiment, but now Scotty's dad was working very hard and Scotty had not seen him in a long while. One day when Scotty was feeling really down about not spending more time with his dad, he went to the wastelands to climb rocks. The hot winds were starting to pick up, and Scotty hoped that a wind storm was not on the way.

Just as he was wondering how to get his dad to take some time off and hang out with him he spotted Aldy playing his syth, off in the distance, beside a big yellow rock. Running as fast as he could, panting and trying to catch his breath, he yelled, "Hey Aldy! What've you been up to?"

"My family was very busy. I had to be at all the family events," Aldy yelled.

"Why's your family so busy?" Scotty asked as he got to where Aldy was sitting.

"Um . . . um . . . oh . . . my father just knows a lot of people. He's involved in all sorts of community activities."

Scotty wondered why Aldy's father knew so many people. Scotty's dad only seemed to know the other scientists whom he worked with at the earthbase.

"Hey, my dad's been really busy lately. I have tons of free time. Do you want to hang out?"

"Sure."

"I brought all kinds of cool stuff in my backpack."

Scotty pulled out a small, shiny, black oval device with a little opening on one end and tiny red, blue, yellow and gold buttons of various shapes all over the top of the oval.

"What is that?"

"It's an Aptec. It's capable of producing all sorts of holograms and virtual reality experiences."

"Earth is so beautiful! I want to show you what my planet looks like."

Scotty pushed a combination of buttons on the Aptec and there, in front of them, hanging in the desert air was a beautiful image of Earth spinning on its axis.

"You've got to come and visit sometime."

"It is so blue! Really a water planet."

Earth sparkled and danced in the air before them. Scotty pushed more buttons on the oval object and zoomed in.

"See the beautiful high mountains with snow-capped peaks?"

"Magnificent! And look at all the animals and plants."

"Here, I'll zip into Old California."

"What are those monster trees called?"

"Redwoods and Sequoias."

Then with the push of a special button the earth image morphed into a beautiful garden in front of a modest little house.

"Where are we now? What are those beautiful red flowers?"

"My mom's garden. She plants roses. They smell awesome!"

Scotty wanted to share everything about Earth with Aldy.

"There are tons of animals that live on the land and in the oceans." And with that Scotty pushed a sequence of buttons and suddenly the boys were surrounded by the walls of a small submarine that was transporting them through the depths of the ocean as they whooshed past whales, green sea turtles and dolphins.

Scotty pushed more buttons and suddenly the pair was exploring a forest full of bears and wolves.

"What are those things with all the legs?"

"They're spiders. They spin webs and catch bugs in the webs and eat them."

"Whoa! What are those beautiful flying creatures?"

"Butterflies."

All at once, the buddies were on safari in Old Africa watching lions, elephants and zebras.

"There are so many different animals on Earth."

"Yep, and the very best animals of all are dogs. I have two dogs, Cody and Sammy. Cody is a husky and Sammy is a collie."

Scotty pulled out his little paper-thin flexible minicomputer from his backpack, unrolled it, and showed Aldy videos of Sammy and Cody playing in his rose-filled yard at home.

"There are very few animals on Kestrellia because it is mostly wastelands and high, bitter, cold mountains. There are no dogs or cats on Kestrellia. The only pets we have are baryas."

"Baryas?"

"Yes, they're fat and furry, but small, about 24 inches high and they have pointy, furry ears and big, round, dark-blue eyes. They are the color of amber, and they can walk on all fours or on their hind legs, and they have little furry hands with four fingers."

"Wow, cool, I want to see one." Scotty was not finished telling Aldy about earth. "There're also all sorts of different people on earth, too."

Scotty pushed more buttons on the Aptec and the boys were surrounded by Africans, Indians, Asians, Native Americans, Latinos and lots more.

"Everybody looks so different! Awesome!"

Aldy was fascinated because there were only two kinds of Kestrellians. "There are only Cerulians like myself and the Larians like Zillian."

"And the Larians are so different from you. Zillian has the longest aqua hair I've ever seen. It goes all the way down to her feet. Her feathery silver eyelashes are really long, too. Plus, she has that wild pale green skin, and it must be so cool to have three arms. Think of all the things you could do at the same time with three arms!"

"Yes, the Larians can do so many things at the same time that we creatures with only two arms can't do."

The two boys met in the barren wastelands for the next two days, played the syth, talked about everything under the sun and stayed until way past the two suns had set. Evenings they gazed at the stars and three Kestrellian moons.

## CHAPTER 3

# THE STORM

The next day Aldy did not come out to the wastelands. Scotty wondered if Aldy was sick or if his family was busy again.

After that Scotty would get up early, say goodbye to his dad as he left for work and then eat breakfast. After sending subspace messages to his mom, and helping Zillian with chores, Scotty made the trek to the wastelands every day and stayed late into the lonely nights, hoping that Aldy would be there. Night after night he waited for his friend. He even braved a wind storm one night hoping that Aldy would come back.

That night, Scotty stayed way too long in the wastelands. He could hear the wind getting closer and closer. He could feel a change in the air and see that dust was beginning to swirl up from the ground and block out Kestrellia's three moons, but he thought, if I just stay a few minutes more maybe Aldy will show up.

The wind picked up and Scotty wondered if he should run for home or stay put.

The wind became violent. Scotty was nearly blown over a couple of times. "Geez, what was I thinking? The wind can blow hundreds of miles an hour during these storms. I should have made a break for home while I still had time." Scotty was getting scared enough to talk to himself for the bit of comfort that somehow offered.

There was lightning with this storm, too. Powerful red lightning shot through circular purple lightning that accompanied Kestrellian wind storms. It terrified Scotty. He had heard that the red lightning could burn a hole in solid rock.

Why did I stay so long tonight? He thought. He could smell the ozone as the lightning crashed through the air. It struck right in front of him at one point.

"I better get behind one of these big boulders and wait this thing out," he whispered to himself.

As the lightning crashed about him and rose from the ground all around him to meet the lightning that flew through the air, it hurt his ears. It was so bright, the night sky lit up, and he had to shut his eyes a few times.

Oh, why did I stay so long? What was I thinking? Aldy has not come out here in days. I may never see him again. The wind is kicking up so much dust! It's getting in my eyes and nose and my throat and choking me!

Suddenly, the thunder sounded different to Scotty. Is that still thunder or do I hear something howling now? There, my mind is making me crazy again!

Scotty clung close to the boulder and shut his eyes praying that the storm would soon move out.

After what seemed like forever Scotty heard the thunder moving off in the distance. He made a break for it. He ran as fast as he could, back to the safety of the earthbase, his home away from home.

Scotty ran for the moving walkway that he knew would take him directly to his little house. He jumped off the walkway, sped to the green front door and threw it open with such force he almost knocked over Zillian, who had been waiting behind the door for him.

"Where have you been? Your father has been home for hours. We were about to call base security and have them go out looking for you."

Scotty could hear his father hurrying down the long dark hallway from the back of the house.

"Son, what happened, where were you?"

"I was out in the desert and I guess, well, I guess I didn't notice the storm coming and before I knew it the wind was howling and I was surrounded by lightning."

Scotty's dad put his arm around his son's shoulders and led him over to the big, oversized brown, cushiony couch in the brightly lit living room while Zillian went to get some dinner for Scotty.

"Well, you're here and you're safe and that's all that matters now. You've got to watch out for those wind storms. We've been studying them at the lab. Nothing like them on Earth. They can be deadly."

Zillian brought a big bowl of hot soup.

"My favorite! Chicken noodle soup, thanks for making this!"

Scotty spent the rest of the evening sitting on the couch with his dad, talking about geology, drinking soup and trying to forget the storm.

Even though the storm had terrified Scotty he still came back every night looking for his friend. Then, late one night just before Scotty was going to head for home, Aldy appeared. It was obvious to Scotty that something was wrong, very wrong.

## CHAPTER 4

# THE QUEST

"Aldy, I was worried about you. Your antennae are drooping! Are you okay?"

"Scotty, I just had my tenth birthday."

"That's great, Aldy. Congratulations! Did you have a party?"

"No, you do not understand, Scotty. No party. It was a solemn occasion. On this planet when the son of the . . . of the . . ."

". . . of the what?"

"Of the ruler, the king, turns ten, it's time for him to start out on The Quest."

"Wait a minute. The ruler of the planet? The Quest? What are you talking about?"

"I should have told you when I first met you. My father is the ruler of the planet, the king of all of Kestrellia."

Now it was starting to make sense. Now Scotty realized that Zillian *did* recognize Aldy, and he

21

understood why Zillian had treated the two boys like royalty when he brought Aldy home for dinner.

"Why didn't you tell me before?"

"I just wanted to be treated like a normal Cerulian boy instead of the future king. I wanted you to be my friend just because you liked me."

"Like you? You're the best syth player I know. And you're the coolest alien I've ever met. You're my best friend, Aldy. That's what I think."

Aldy's antennae perked up. "Finally, I have a real friend, finally, someone I can truly count on."

"You can always, ALWAYS count on me. We're buds! So . . . what's The Quest?"

Aldy took a long, deep breath and began. "It's a very old, ancient, sacred ritual that has to be performed by the oldest son of the ruler when he turns ten. The Quest is a test of courage, strength, intelligence, and endurance. If I do not accomplish The Quest, at my father's death, the crown will pass to the other royal family. If I do not do this, then the next king will be the Larian, called Jessup. He is very different from my father, from me, and the rest of my people. He must not become king. Scotty, Jessup is evil. He is mean and hurts people. It is so important that I find the Blue Kyrolite."

"The blue what?" Scotty asked.

"The Blue Kyrolite is a precious gem. I've heard stories about it being large, translucent, and glowing with an inner light. The high priests of Kestrellia supposedly hid the Blue Kyrolite somewhere in the northern mountains when I was born. I must go on The Quest, find it, and bring it back to the high priests. If I do this the Blue Kyrolite will give me great power, power that will make me a superior ruler."

"The high priests? Who the heck are they?"

"Well, it's hard to say. They are holy men who are believed to be ancient, at least 4,000 years old. It's rumored that they came to Kestrellia from another planet, which makes sense because they don't look like Larians or Cerulians."

"That's weird! So what makes Jessup so bad?"

He wants complete control over everything and everyone. Jessup is afraid of anyone who thinks for him- or herself. He will stop at nothing to have control over Kestrellia. He would murder me and my family so that no one will oppose his rule."

Scotty shook with fear.

"Scotty, I must do The Quest to prove that I am brave, strong, intelligent, and worthy of becoming king. I can take anyone I want on The Quest with me. You are my best friend. Would you come with me to find the Blue Kyrolite?"

Scotty did not know what to say. He stammered, "W-w-well, I don't know."

Here I go again, he thought. I'm always so scared. What if we get lost? What if I break a leg? What if I fall off a mountain? What if there are wild beasts along the way? What if . . .

Scotty could see that Aldy was getting worried. His antennae were drooping more and more with every second Scotty took to make up his mind.

Scotty's mind was filling with wild thoughts. The mountains are distant, and I have not ever been that far away from my home here on Kestrellia. What will my dad say if I tell him I'm going to go to the high mountains in search of some weird jewel? How long will it take? How dangerous will it be? Will anyone help us? Now I can feel my cheeks getting hot again. I am gonna start shaking any minute. I just know it. My heart is beating so fast, it's going to beat right out of my chest. Great, I'll probably start stuttering soon.

Scotty took a deep breath and realized that his father probably would not even know he was gone. He could just tell Zillian he was staying at Aldy's for a few days.

Why shouldn't I help Aldy? He thought. Aldy is my absolute best friend. Aldy should be king. Without my help Aldy might not become king, and Jessup would be the king. That sounds ever scarier than making a trek into the mountains.

"Aldy, I've got it all figured out. I'll tell Zillian I'm staying at your house for a few days, and then no one will wonder where I am. We need to start making plans for your quest."

Aldy was so happy his purple eyes twinkled and his antennae perked way up and twirled in circles.

The boys were going on a great quest.

## CHAPTER 5

# THE START

"So when do we get started?" Scotty asked.

"We can meet at my house after the suns come up. How about nine?"

"Sounds good. What should we bring?"

"Food, water, backpacks, good walking shoes or hiking boots . . ."

". . . clean clothes? Scotty added.

"Yeah, the basics, that's probably all we'll need."

"Okay, well I'm off to get a good night's sleep and tell Zillian that I'll be staying at your house for awhile."

Scotty winked at Aldy and the two boys waved goodbye.

Aldy arrived back at the royal residence a little tired and stressed. Since his family chose to use their money not for themselves, but for their people, Aldy's home was a somewhat modest three-story house for royalty. The magenta house had the appearance of three flying saucers of decreasing size piled on top of each other.

They sat on a base that spread out at the bottom. There were triangular windows around the rim of each saucer and a clear glass staircase wound around the saucers and lead to a small pointed tower where Aldy's father could go when he needed some quiet time. There were smaller versions of the royal house, without the tower, and in different colors, spread over the three acres that made up the royal complex. These smaller houses were for the king's staff and their families.

Aldy ran up the large glass staircase at the bottom of the lowest saucer that led to his big shiny, turquoise metal front door. He pulled the door open and yelled, "Mom, I'm so tired from being in the desert all day. I'm skipping dinner and going to sleep."

Antennae drooping a bit, his mom shook her head and yelled back, "Okay, but if you get hungry later come down, and I'll make you a snack."

Aldy ran into his room, jumped into his small overstuffed round bed and pulled the soft fuzzy gold covers over his head. As Aldy tossed and turned he opened his eyes to see his father standing over him.

"Aldy, the high priests would like to meet with you."

A chill went through Aldy. He slowly got out of bed and was led by his father into his huge conference room with massive black table and big high-backed red-cushioned chairs. The high priests in their creepy robes were sitting around the table. Aldy's father pulled out the chair at the head of the table for Aldy, gave him a concerned look, and silently left the room.

"Aldy, the Blue Kyrolite is very important and very valuable, and The Quest will be the most dangerous and meaningful journey you will ever take in your entire life. If the Blue Kyrolite falls into the wrong hands your life and the lives of millions will be in jeopardy. Kestrellia will become a cursed planet. Remember this, Aldy, the Blue Kyrolite will be hidden to you until you prove you are worthy of finding it."

"But what really is the Blue Kyrolite?"

"It is precious. Search far and wide for it. Search your soul for it."

And with that the mysterious priests jumped up in unison from the table and left the room.

Search my soul for it? Weird, Aldy thought.

When Scotty showed up at Aldy's house he told Scotty about his strange meeting with the high priests.

"I spent the night dreaming about blue gems and those peculiar high priests. It was very disturbing."

Scotty hoped Aldy was worthy of finding the Blue Kyrolite very soon. The high mountains are cold and dangerous, no place for us boys to be spending so much time alone. Scotty shivered at the thought of being in the high mountains for very long. This planet is so strange, nothing but high mountains, lots of desert and a very small green area. He thought about the stories he had heard about devils, trolls, strange beasts and weather that could change in seconds. He was getting butterflies in his stomach at the notion of getting lost up there.

"I wonder if we should have packed more food and water," Scotty asked. "We only packed enough for a few days. We could end up starving to death."

"Scotty, don't worry. I know these mountains so well. We will be fine. I camped in the mountains with my dad and uncles when I was a little boy. It won't take long to find a bright blue gem against the gray rocks of the stark mountains."

It was still early morning when the best friends were ready to start out on The Quest. The king's entire staff and their families and of course the intimidating high priests were all waiting to say goodbye. Scotty thought Aldy's mom had tears in her eyes. The high priests followed the boys outside to the edge of the beautiful flower-filled yard.

"Be strong and brave. Never doubt yourselves. Fear nothing."

Oh sure, never doubt myself, fear nothing, Scotty thought.

The priests continued, "May spirit guide you to a quick and safe return from the high mountains. Peace."

They were spooky figures standing there in the morning sunlight. The high priests were tall, with thin faces and high cheek bones. Their long, flowing hooded silver robes shimmered in the sunlight from the twin suns. Their long white beards were full of crystals that sparkled in the bright morning sun. Their skin was almost translucent.

Scotty could almost see through their skin, but he did not see any veins. Were they androids or some kind of robots?

They encircled the boys and in their deep voices with their strange accents they said, "Seek the truth."

Scotty blurted out. "That's a weird thing to say."

"Yes, weird." Aldy whispered so that high priests could not hear him.

"We're supposed to be searching for a magnificent blue jewel, aren't we?"

"Yes, we are. Not the 'truth' about anything that I can think of," Aldy said quietly.

"Hmmm . . . strange. Bizarre. Really bizarre!"

Aldy's dad, mom, uncles, aunts and baby brother were all outside to see the boys off on their mission to find the shining blue jewel. Aldy's dad looked concerned. He put his arms around his son and gave him a big hug and said, "Be careful, up there. Come back soon."

As the boys left Aldy's house and headed toward the mountains they looked back and waved to everyone.

Aldy's mom was rocking Aldy's baby brother in her arms, trying to quiet him. She looked worried and Scotty was right, there were tears in her eyes. Scotty trembled. Scotty wondered how soon it would be before they all saw each other again.

As they walked away Aldy pointed directly ahead. "The best trail for us to start out on is that well-worn trail straight ahead. I hiked that trial many times on camping trips."

The trail seemed to rise up for miles and miles ahead of them. It was cut on the side of a steep cliff. On one side rose the mountains and on the other side was a sheer, rocky drop off into an ever-deepening valley below.

It was a chilly morning, but the two suns of Kestrellia were rising. It would soon be warm and sunny. The boys talked and laughed in anticipation of finding the great blue prize. They stopped for lunch by a small rare mountain stream with clear water and red rocks covering the bottom. It made the most soothing sound, calming Scotty's overactive nerves.

"Scotty, I'm remembering stories I heard about Jessup's great-grandfather. He did some very bad things way before I was born, when he was king. He started wars on Kestrellia, but I cannot remember the details right now."

After lunch the boys left the pretty little peaceful stream and headed further into the tall, jagged mountains that seemed to be looming over them. The mountains appeared threatening to Scotty, who especially took note of the tall rock formations he had spotted in the higher elevations. They looked almost alive.

"Those tall, thin pyramids of black rock, jutting out between the peaks, what are they?"

"We call them witch's wands. They are made of rough sandstone and have tiny purple crystals imbedded in the sandstone. How they were formed is a mystery."

Witch's Wands! Great! Just what my crazy mind needs to hear. Scotty thought to himself, just keep hiking, keep your mind on the trail, one foot in front of the other, one foot in front of the other. Don't let Aldy see how scared you are.

Aldy had said he could spot the Blue Kyrolite quickly, so he and Scotty concentrated on that while they hiked in silence. Scotty pondered the deep valley the trail was following off to the right.

"Aldy, that valley to the right of us is really, really deep. What if we fall into it?"

"Scotty, you're so funny sometimes. Gravity will keep us on the trail, do not worry, my friend. This part of the trail is wide and not too slippery, and gravity will keep our feet firmly planted on the trail."

That did not help Scotty much since his mind was off and running again. He imagined tumbling down the side of the jagged cliff and into the deep, dark valley below. Splat! Scotty shuddered and imagined himself dead in a million pieces with no one to find his rotting bones for days, animals picking at his eyeballs. UGH! Scotty shivered. What gruesome thoughts I have.

"I'll feel better when this trail makes a turn through the mountains, and I don't have to look down this valley anymore," he muttered to Aldy.

After a while Scotty felt tired and noticed the suns were sinking.

"Aldy, we've been hiking for hours. I think it's getting late."

Aldy's concentration was broken, and as he looked around he said, "We've been out here all day with no sign of the Blue Kyrolite. We will have to camp out here tonight and continue up into the higher elevations tomorrow."

Luckily the boys were near a small cave that would make a nice, cozy campsite for the night. They built a fire with the firesticks that Aldy had packed. Although Scotty knew that they were not really magic, and that they worked according to some science that he did not understand, Scotty thought they were almost magic. They looked like purple crayons. All you had to do was break them, throw them on the ground, and a fire would spark up.

The boys settled down in their cozy cave by their toasty fire. Just as Scotty was about the fall asleep he heard the strangest noise: "Riff, riff, riff, riff."

"I don't believe it," Aldy said.

"What is it?"

"A wild barya. Some barya came to live with us years ago as pets and others stayed in these mountains."

"Are they dangerous? Do they bite? Do they have claws or fangs? Do they spray poison?"

"Ha, ha, ha . . . no . . . ha, ha, ha . . . they're harmless. They are usually more scared of us than we are of them. The barya will stay away from us when they spot the fire."

That put Scotty's mind at ease for awhile until his next attack of fear and panic. He and Aldy curled up in their sleeping bags and fell fast asleep.

## CHAPTER 6

# BABIES AND GHOSTS

Early in the morning as the two suns were just rising, a sliver of light brightened the cave. Scotty woke, slowly rolled over in his sleeping bag, and came face to face with a tiny baby barya. He was fat, fuzzy, about 13 inches high and his big, round, dark-blue eyes were staring at Scotty. Scotty's heart started pounding.

"Aldy, Aldy! Wake up! We have a visitor!"

Aldy awoke and laughed. "He must have wandered away from his family. We'll take him with us today and hopefully along the way he will find his family."

Scotty thought he looked like a little fat roly poly bear cub. The barya put his little furry four-fingered hand in Aldy's, looked at him with his big blue eyes and said, "Al-dy."

Scotty jumped up out of his sleeping bag. "They can talk?"

"Yep."

"Hey, my name is Scotty."

"Scot-ty?"

"Yeah, that's right. This is so cool! A little bear creature that can speak English. I can't wait to tell my dad about this."

The two best friends ate breakfast, rolled up their sleeping bags, packed their backpacks, and off they traveled with the baby barya riding on Aldy's shoulders.

Aldy and Scotty were hiking for hours, going higher and higher into the mountains, constantly searching everywhere along the trail and examining every peak for the blue jewel. But after exploring for hours they found no gem and no family of baryas so they could not drop off the little baby. It was getting colder the higher they climbed, and the wind was picking up.

Scotty's fingers and nose were getting cold and he shivered. "I . . . I . . . wish we had packed some cold-weather clothes because it's getting awfully chilly."

"I wish we had, too, but I never thought we would be climbing so high into the mountains to find the Blue Kyrolite. I cannot believe the high priests hid it so far up in these mountains."

The boys were getting cold and frustrated. The baby barya wanted to play, running in and out between their legs while they hiked, but the boys were on a mission to find the Blue Kyrolite.

Finally Aldy said, "It looks like we're going to have to spend another night out in these mountains."

"Okay, no problem," Scotty replied. "Anything for a friend and anything for the future king of Kestrellia."

Scotty wanted to sound brave for his friend, but his mind was starting to race. He thought, Geez, I hope Aldy can't tell how scared I'm getting.

Scotty was getting a queasy feeling in his stomach again, and he could feel his cheeks getting hot. What if we get lost and can't find our way back for days and days? We could be starving to death and some horrible gross monster could find us half dead from lack of food and eat us for *his* dinner. I'd never see my dad and mom again. My dogs would always wonder why I never came home. I'd never see Earth again! Yipes! There goes my crazy mind again. Yipes!

The boys found some shelter under a rock ledge and made camp for the night. Now little Barty, that is what Scotty was calling the barya, could run around and play while the boys ate dinner. They were so exhausted. They decided to go to sleep right after dinner so they could get an early start the next morning. Curled up in their sleeping bags, they tried to get warm while the wind howled around them. Their new little barya friend curled up in Scotty's sleeping bag.

The boys had a rough night. It was cold and hard to sleep and the rock ledge did not offer much protection from the howling wind. They both had strange dreams about blue gems and high priests that woke them up from time to time. Scotty also dreamed about monsters: horrible beasts with horns and yellow fangs and long sharp claws that could slash and rip the two of them to pieces while they innocently slept. He dreamed that these hideous beasts were hiding in the mountains where they could not be seen until it was too late.

The next morning after the nightmares were over the boys got up, ate a small breakfast, and decided to get an early start.

Aldy said, "I sure didn't get much sleep last night, did you?"

"Nope, and it's so early. The suns aren't even up yet."

"I know, but we really need to get going and try to hike as high as possible today."

The boys started hiking just as both suns were coming up over the craggy, intimidating peaks. Higher and higher they went, always scanning nooks and crannies in the mountains for the blue gem.

"I'm so tired!"

"We have got to keep going."

"I know . . . I know. The higher we climb, the colder it gets. How many feet to do you think we climbed so far this morning?"

"Probably a good 500."

"Five hundred! We're moving faster than I thought we were."

"Yes, 500 and still no Blue Kyrolite in sight."

"We've been going nonstop for hours. I'm getting hungry."

"Me, too. We should look for a place where we can stop and have lunch. Hey, how about over there." Aldy pointed toward what looked like a little cave. After a quick lunch in the cold, dark cave, they climbed higher. The trail became more rugged and harder to follow.

They slipped and went sliding backward a few times, but luckily caught each other. Scotty was starting to let his crazy thoughts get the best of him again. "That was close. For a moment I thought I was gonna go off the side."

Aldy shook his head. "I would never let that happen to you."

After they hiked another hundred feet, up ahead Scotty could see that the trail went under an enormously high waterfall that started hundreds of feet up in the mountains. I'll bet that water is really cold, Scotty thought. I'm going to freeze walking under that waterfall. I'll start shivering, and my lips will turn blue, I might get sick, I won't get back to the lowlands in time to get the medical care I need, and I'll die up here in these miserable mountains.

Just as the boys reached the waterfall, and Scotty was pondering death from the most horrible flu he had ever had in his entire nine years, his right foot slipped on the wet trail and it slid over the edge of trail. Scotty was half on the trail and half off and trying desperately to grab onto something, anything and not completely slip off the trail and into the jaws of the deep, dark valley below.

This is it Scotty thought, this is the way I'm going to die. Just as I suspected, I'll plunge down to the valley below and some huge ugly beast will be sucking the marrow out of my bones for his beastly dinner tonight.

"Oh, n–n–no!" he shouted as he tried to get hold of the wet rocks that covered the trail. Barty was shrieking, "Scot-ty, Scot-ty!"

Aldy heard the commotion and turned to see his friend with half of his body off the trail, dangling precariously over the side. He ran to Scotty and grabbed him with his long arms and hands and hoisted him back on the trail.

"See, I told you I would never let you go off the edge. Are you all right?"

Shaken, Scotty replied, "I . . . I . . . I'm okay."

"Sorry, my friend," Aldy said, "I forgot to mention that gravity will keep your feet on a *dry* trail!"

The boys laughed, and after Scotty caught his breath the two of them had both feet firmly planted on the ground and were once again hiking further up into the cold, gray mountains. After hiking for another hour the moment Scotty had been waiting for finally arrived: The trail made a turn through the mountains and away from the spooky valley below. Scotty breathed a sigh of relief.

Aldy turned to Scotty and said, "I bet you feel better now."

"You better believe I do. Although now that the trail has cut straight through the mountains it's sure gotten really steep."

"It'll get steeper and steeper now. It may slow us down a bit."

They spent hours slowly climbing higher and higher and scanning the towering peaks for a blue gem sparkling in the sunlight, but before they knew it, the suns were setting again, bringing another night outside high up in those lonely mountains. They made camp in an area surrounded by high brush with a little rock ledge to sleep under, ate a little of what was left in their backpacks, and decided to try to go to sleep early. They were all so tired, even Barty seemed exhausted.

The Kestrellian moons cast an eerie glow over the mountains and the wind howled and howled. Or was it the wind or an alien werewolf? Scotty thought. Scotty could not sleep. He tossed and turned and finally he could not take it anymore. "Aldy, Aldy, wake up!"

Aldy woke up slowly. He was so tired he just mumbled, "What? What is it, Scotty? You all right?"

"Listen! Listen to that howling! Is that an animal?"

"No animal I know. It's just the wind."

But just as Aldy said that, tales he had heard years before came rushing back. "I remember being told stories when I was a little kid about the mountains being haunted by the ghosts of Kestrellians who had lost their way up here and never returned to the lowlands."

"Hey, don't listen to me. It's nothing, my friend, just the wind. It sometimes gets stronger at night in these higher elevations. We should just go back to sleep."

Aldy's words calmed Scotty. He fell back to sleep for a little while, but Aldy lay awake listening to the howling. He suddenly jumped up.

"Scotty, wake up!"

"What's wrong?"

"Now I'm wondering if the stories of ghosts are true. Suddenly, all the ghost stories I heard came rushing back to me. I'm remembering tales about gruesome ghosts with long, skinny arms and cold, bony fingers with sharp pointy yellow nails. They materialize out of nowhere and fly at you with the speed of light. They can strangle you with their long bony fingers. They can suck your soul out through the top of your head when their hideous green eyes lock onto yours."

Scotty was sorry Aldy was telling him this. Scotty could almost feel their cold bony fingers around his neck and their sharp pointy nails digging deep into his skin. He could feel his soul, his spirit, his essence being slowly and painfully drained from every part of his body while it was sucked out through the top of his head.

Scotty let out a deep sigh. There goes my mind, racing again, imagining the worst again. He tried to sound brave, "Aldy, that's just a story, go to sleep. We're going to need all the sleep we can get. I don't even hear the wind howling anymore."

Aldy visibly relaxed into his sleeping bag. "Okay, thanks for calming me down."

Out of sheer exhaustion the boys finally fell asleep with Barty curled up between them.

## CHAPTER 7

# THE CLIMB

Early in the morning before the suns rose in the sky, a very scared Barty woke them.

"Riff, riff, riff, riff, riiiffffffff! Scotttttt-ttttty! Allllll-ddddddddy!"

"What's wrong?"

"There must be a tigarus close by."

"A what?"

"Tigari are the only other furry animals besides barya that live in the mountains. Tigari are large, about double the size of the earth wolves you were telling me about, black with red spots, big pointy purple ears, and intense yellow eyes. They're pretty harmless, but baryas are leery of them because they are so big and can really move fast when they're on the hunt for their favorite food, the peonee."

"Peonee?"

"Something like a cross between a tall, spiny cactus and a small tree. A hungry tigarus, with its massive, strong jaws can devour a huge peonee in just a few bites, and they're so-oo-oo fast! They can easily outrun any Kestrellian, Larian, or Cerulian!"

Scotty said, "I think we better stay under this rock ledge for awhile and be quiet while we eat breakfast. Hopefully, the tigarus will pass through here quickly."

Even though Aldy said the tigarus was harmless Scotty's mind was racing. What if this was a mutant tigarus that liked human flesh instead of peonees? What if it had a keen sense of smell and could easily smell them? What if it could not find any peonees? Would it settle for a little earthboy for breakfast instead? What if . . . what if . . . WHAT IF WHAT? I wish sometimes I could just tell my mind to shut up. Scotty put his arm around Barty to calm him, but it was also to calm himself. He tried to concentrate on eating breakfast, but it was difficult; he could hardly swallow the food, and his stomach was feeling queasy again.

Luckily the tigarus moved quickly and was gone before Scotty's mind could create more crazy fantasies. The boys packed their belongings and headed out again farther up through the mountains, farther, Scotty thought, toward *The Truth*.

Hmmm . . . Scotty thought, I must really be losing it. What did that mean, "further toward The Truth"? Where had that wild thought come from?

After hiking a while longer Scotty said, "Aldy, the strangest thoughts are popping into my head."

"Like what?"

"The phrase 'The Truth' keeps popping into my head. Remember, like what the high priests told you?"

Aldy stopped dead in his tracks. "Scotty, you know I've been having strange thoughts, too. What if we're really not supposed to find a beautiful blue gem shining in the mountains? What if that's just a way for the priests to describe something else that we're on a quest for?"

Just as Aldy was trying to figure out what the high priest's strange words could possibly mean something high up on a very tall witch's wand caught his eye.

"Scotty! I see it! THE BLUE KYROLITE!"

"Where?"

"About a hundred feet up that witch's wand. We have got to climb up there."

Scotty's eyes followed to where Aldy's long finger was pointing. He was completely terrified. The wand was tall, rough and it was a very windy day. Scotty had never climbed anything like that before, and with the wind whipping around it would be treacherous. It would be easy for Aldy, he was taller, he had longer legs and arms and Cerulains had skinny feet that could fit into little holes and grooves in the rocks. I'm so small, especially for my age. I'm so scared! What if I slip? What if I get to the top and fall off?

Scotty was trembling. He could feel his cheeks getting hot and figured they were probably bright red, too. His palms were sweating. Oh geez, he thought, that will make it hard for me to get a handhold when I'm climbing the awful witch's wand. His heart was starting to pound out of his chest. What am I gonna do? I can't let Aldy know how scared I am. I can't let Aldy down. I have to be brave and climb up there with him. What if the Blue Kyrolite is stuck between two rocks or something, and Aldy needs help getting it out? What if Aldy slips, and I have to help him? I have to be brave. I can do this! Scotty took a deep breath and said in a shaky voice, "You . . . you . . . you go first, Aldy, and I'll follow behind you."

"Okay!"

Aldy took off fast up the witch's wand as if he was born to climb, just as Scotty had suspected he would. Scotty gingerly grabbed the first handhold he could find on the wand's surface and slowly and carefully started working his way up the wand. He climbed at a snail's pace because the rocks were even sharper than he had expected.

"Ouch!" he muttered to himself so Aldy could not hear him. "These rocks are cutting my hands to pieces. Ouch! That really hurts!" He groaned. He was not even halfway there yet.

Aldy was so far ahead, Scotty could hardly see him. Scotty was breathing heavily, and his mind was starting to take off as usual. The wand felt like it was covered with tiny sharp needles and sandpaper.

Scotty was mentally going over the jam he was in and trying to concentrate on what he could do so he could get to the top of the wand. My hands hurt, and it's getting harder and harder to hold on. I don't think I'm going to make it, but I've got to keep trying. I just have to be really careful about each new rock I grab as I climb, and I have to carefully take hold of the rocks so I don't get any more cuts. Just be careful, be careful, Scotty, old boy, don't do anything foolish, he told himself.

The wind was whipping around the wand. It kept blowing Scotty's blond curls in his face as he tried to look for rocks and handholds to grasp.

Scotty looked up and thought, I can't believe how far ahead of me Aldy is getting. I've got to try to catch up. Ouch! Scotty slammed his knee against a rock. It felt bruised and he was sure it was bleeding. Scotty tried to stretch his arms as far as he could and pull himself up the wand faster and faster so he could catch up to Aldy. He was sweating and gasping for breath.

Scotty stopped for a minute and made the mistake of looking back down the wand for a second. He saw how far he had climbed. It scared him. He was so high! He was about 50 feet off the ground, and it was dizzying. He lost his balance and his foothold, and started sliding down the wand. He was trying desperately to hold onto something, anything he could grab to slow his fall, but he kept falling, falling, falling.

He hit the ground with a thud and fell in a heap at the bottom of the witch's wand. He was dazed for a minute. Barty was so worried about Scotty, he came running over and jumped in his lap and was running his little furry hands all over Scotty's face in an effort to comfort him.

"Scot–ty, Scot–ty, okay?"

Clutching Barty, upset with himself for being so clumsy, shaking, sweating, heart pounding, mind racing, Scotty sat there exhausted, waiting for Aldy to return with the Blue Kyrolite. He was so incredibly, unbelievably exhausted. There not an ounce of energy left in his small body, and then something amazing happened.

# CHAPTER 8

# REAL MONSTERS

"Scotty, Scotty are you all right? Scotty, can you hear me? Scotty! Scotty!" Aldy was holding Scotty by the shoulders and shaking him. "Scotty, snap out of it! Scotty what is wrong with you? Scotty, can you hear me? Scotty look at me, can you see me?"

Aldy was terrified. He had never seen Scotty act like this before.

Scotty shook his head and looked at Aldy as though he had just seen him for the first time. He could hardly speak, "Y-ye-yesss, I can hear you. I can see you."

"Are you all right? What happened? You were staring at me, but it seemed as though you really could not see me standing here right in front of you."

"Aldy! The most amazing thing just happened! My mind stopped!"

"What?"

"I guess because I was so exhausted after the fall, my mind just stopped racing, it stopped spinning in circles. My mind was so tired from the climb and the fall. It couldn't create all its stories for awhile. It was calm, peaceful. It was still for the first time in my life! I didn't have a crazy thought in my head for the first time in my nine years! I felt total peace! Total peace! It's a miracle! Aldy, my whole life my mind has been running nonstop, making up stories about everything and everybody, creating monsters where there were none and making me afraid of everything and everybody. I was even afraid of you when I first saw you in the wastelands."

Aldy laughed. "I'm no one to be afraid of."

Suddenly, Scotty remembered why he had been climbing that awful witch's wand. "Oh, geez, yipes! Aldy! I almost forgot! Where's the Blue Kyrolite?"

Aldy's antennae drooped. "There was no Blue Kyrolite up there. All this for nothing. When I got to the place where I had seen something shining there was nothing but a small patch of crystal minerals that were reflecting the sunlight."

"Too bad!"

"Scotty, your hands!"

Due to all the excitement Scotty had managed to block out the pain. Scotty looked down at his hands and suddenly realized that they hurt really badly. They were covered with dozens of small cuts that were bleeding.

"Scotty, put your hands in mine."

What a weird request, Scotty thought, but he trusted his friend so he put his small hands in Aldy's long, thin, graceful ones. Aldy held Scotty's swollen, bleeding hands with his long fingers and pressed his round flat silver nails against Scotty's hands. Quickly, Scotty felt his hands becoming very warm and there was a faint glow coming from Aldy's fingertips.

"Whoa! Th-th-the cuts are gone! They just disappeared!"

"Scotty, you hurt your knee, too. It's very red and swollen."

"I slammed it against a rock while I was trying to catch up to you."

Scotty watched in amazement while Aldy's fingertips glowed as they touched his knee and slowly the swelling, redness, and bruising went away–completely.

"How did you do that?"

"Cerulians are healers."

"Healers? You never told me that."

"It's not a big deal."

"Maybe not to you. You always surprise me. This planet is full of surprises." Then it hit Scotty again. "Geez, we still haven't found that gem."

Disappointed, the boys sat at the base of the witch's wand for a long time trying to decide what to do next. After a while the boys just settled back while Barty slept curled up on the ground.

"I'm tired."

"Me, too." Muttered Scotty. "Should we keep climbing? What if the high priests really didn't hide something real, something solid for you to find?"

The boys sat there at the base of the rock wand, cold, shivering, tired and starting to lose track of time.

"Scotty how many days have we been up here?"

"I don't know for sure. Days and nights are starting to blend together. I'm not sure anymore if we've been gone from home for two nights, or three, or more."

Aldy added, "You know our supply of food and water was already too low. We cannot go on much longer."

Finally Scotty said, "You know, Aldy, we won't be kids forever. Someday we'll be grownups. This quest is to prepare you to be a grownup king, right?"

"Right."

Scotty thought for a minute and then said, "Well then, somehow, some way we've got to figure out what's going on. Is there really a Blue Kyrolite? If so, where is it?"

"You really are the best friend for me," Aldy said. "You are absolutely right. Maybe it's time for me to start growing up. I mean really growing up: becoming a responsible grownup who can lead my people. What was it I heard about Jessup's great-grandfather a long time ago? I'm so tired. I can't think right now."

"Let's make camp early tonight, build a fire, and rest. We can play with Barty and just have some fun for awhile."

"Sounds good."

Good, no more climbing. Scotty was happy. His legs had started to ache at the end of every day and he was tired, too, so very tired. Just as Scotty was starting to picture that peaceful evening ahead of them, a shrieking scream filled the air.

"W-w-what's that?" Scotty murmured.

"It is a tirradon!"

"Tirra . . . what?"

Aldy excitedly explained, "They are one of the few flying creatures on Kestrellia. They live in the high craggy peaks. They have a 30-foot wingspan and a body covered with dark green and black shiny skin."

"Are you kidding me?"

"No, they also have large whip-like tails that are covered with spikes from the beginning to the pointy end, and they have enormous pointy heads."

"Yipes!" Scotty gasped.

"They have the deepest, blackest eyes I have ever seen and large red fangs and worst of all . . . they breathe fire!"

Scotty was horrified. "Why didn't you tell me about Tirradons?"

"They are so rare most Kestrellians never get to see one in a lifetime."

Just my luck Scotty thought. I get to see a tirradon in *my* lifetime. Scotty's mind was off and running. He thought, I just know this is how I'm going to die. The tirradon will aim his fiery breath right at me. I just know it! He could feel its hot breath on his skin, he could feel his skin melting away. His heart was pounding again. He was trembling.

Fumes were suddenly burning his nose. He could smell the nasty, disgusting, toxic fumes from burning rock as the tirradon's fiery breath hit the mountains.

Just then the tirradon's ghastly screech echoed through the mountains again.

Scotty yelled, "Run!" and took off.

Aldy yelled back, "I saw a cave around the bend from the witch's wand while I was climbing."

"Then let's head for the cave. C'mon, Barty, run!"

Barty jumped on Aldy's shoulders, and the boys took off for the cave. They ran as fast as they could, faster and faster while the tirradon chased after them. Scotty was so frightened he did not pay attention when he ran into the cave; he just ran and ran as fast as he could so he could get as far in the cave as possible, hoping that if he ran really far in, the hot breath of the tirradon could not reach him. Horrified, Scotty suddenly realized he had run too far in. He was lost.

"Ut . . . oh, where have I run to?" He whispered to himself. I can't hear Aldy and Barty. It's so dark I can't see my hand in front of my face. How do I get out of here? Scotty was panicking. He was shaking with fear. Maybe if I'm really quiet for a minute I'll hear Aldy or Barty and be able to find my way back to them. If only my heart would stop pounding, and I could stop breathing so hard I could hear my friends. Oh, why, why, why does everything scare me so much? I wish

I could stop my mind right now. I wish it would just stop spinning like after my fall from the witch's wand, but it won't stop and I can't make it stop. I could die in this cave!

Slowly, Scotty thought he was starting to feel like something was touching him. He was sure he could feel hundreds of hands on his shoulders, on his legs, on his arms. Alien hands of all shapes and sizes: fat ones, skinny ones, hands with four fingers, hands with seven fingers, hands with pointy nails. They seemed to be turning him in all directions, 'round and 'round in circles.

Is this my runaway imagination getting the best of me again? He asked himself. If I could stop my mind for just one minute, just like after I fell off the witch's wand, I could find my way out of here.

Scotty was imaging arms and hands coming out of the cave walls, turning him in all directions. He was even getting dizzy, his head was spinning, and he was getting queasy from being turned 'round and 'round and 'round.

Just as he thought he could not stand it anymore he heard something.

"Riff, riff. Find Scot-ty."

Scotty was so happy. Barty came running out of nowhere and jumped up into Scotty's arms while Aldy came running up behind him.

"I wasn't sure we were going to find you, but since baryas have such a keen sense of smell and they can see heat signatures from other living beings in the dark, we did."

"I didn't have a clue where I was. I thought I'd never find my way out. Wow, these barya aren't just the cute, cuddly little creatures I thought they were."

Kestrellia was full of surprises, sometimes too full of surprises, Scotty thought.

"We're pretty far in. Barty can lead us out. Barty, lead the way!" Aldy instructed.

The boys followed Barty's "riff, riff, riff" and "fol-low, fol-low" to the mouth of the cave.

"What a day!"

"We need to find a place to make camp."

"Definitely!"

The boys made camp under a huge, rare stand of dalix trees that provided great shelter for them and the little baby barya. They were very tall and their thick branches spread out in all directions, forming a great canopy for the boys to camp under. The dalix leaves were huge; each leaf was twelve inches long and a deep crimson color with purple veins. The trunks of the trees were about ten feet around and the bark was deep orange and shiny.

"The birds on Earth would love to roost in these trees. Too bad there are no birds on Kestrellia unless we want to count those flying monsters as birds."

"Ha, ha, ha, I guess that is the only thing that could pass for a bird on Kestrellia."

"Why are there no birds on Kestrellia?"

"Something happened a long time ago, and they disappeared."

"Like what?"

"It had something to do with Jessup's grandfather and war, but I don't remember all the details."

"This is a very strange planet, Aldy."

"Yes, but it is my home."

Scotty and Aldy made a great fire, pulled out some of the last bits of food and water they had, and settled in for the night. After dinner the boys sat watching the flames dancing while their minds raced.

"How big is the Blue Kyrolite?" Scotty asked.

"I don't know."

"What shape is it? What shade of blue is it?"

"Not sure."

"Why haven't we found it yet? Are we really supposed to be on a quest for a blue gem? If not, what are we really supposed to be looking for?"

Scotty thought about how scary the trip had been so far. What was going to be waiting for them tomorrow, huge spiders that paralyzed you with their poison and then ripped your heart out and chewed off your head? Bug-eyed monsters that dissolved your skin with acid that oozed from their hideous claws? Snakes the size of a football field that could suck your brains out? He really wished they would find that blue jewel already. Exhausted by his thoughts Scotty finally fell asleep and joined Aldy and baby Barty who were already in dreamland.

## CHAPTER 9

# STILLNESS

By the time the boys got up the next morning the yellow and orange suns were high in the sky.

"Wow! We really overslept."

"Yeah, we better skip breakfast and get going. Half the morning is gone already. We need to climb higher today."

They packed as fast as they could, and as Barty jumped up on Aldy's shoulder the boys took off for the higher elevations.

"How far do you think we should hike today?"

"About two miles. We'll gain about 400 feet in elevation along the way."

"It's getting colder as we go."

"Yes, it will get colder and colder now, almost bitterly freezing at times."

"The faster we walk and the harder the climb the more we'll keep warm, I guess," Scotty muttered to himself.

After hiking for a couple of hours Scotty noticed that the trail made a sharp bend. "I wonder what's around that bend," he said casually to Aldy.

"That bend in the trail looks familiar to me for some reason," Aldy said.

The trail made almost a 90-degree bend around a high rock wall so it was nearly impossible to see where the trail was going. As the boys cleared the bend, Aldy said, "I recognize this area, Scotty. My dad and I camped here years ago with my uncles when I was about six." They hiked about a quarter of mile further. Suddenly Aldy started running ahead.

He yelled back to Scotty, "I think . . . I think . . . yes! I see it! Yes! Yes! There it is!" He was waving his arms toward a beautiful frozen blue, circular lake, right around the bend, the body of water was ringed by high jagged peaks.

"I remember the wonderful times we had here. Scotty, I can't believe we found this lake. I had so much fun here years ago!"

And with that Aldy took off running faster and faster toward the lake. Aldy's antennae were dancing in circles as he ran and ran and ran slipping and sliding the whole way . . . right out toward the middle of the *frozen* lake.

"Aldy, be careful! It's summer! That ice probably isn't very thick. The ice might be really, really thin!"

But Aldy could not hear his friend. He had run really far ahead of Scotty, and all he could see was the beautiful lake where he had so much fun years ago.

Slipping, sliding, gliding and skidding across the lake, Aldy went as he continued out to the middle, and then it happened.

The ice gave way under Aldy and through it he went, into the freezing waters. Scotty gasped, and cried, "Oh no! Aldy! Aldy! OH NO!"

What neither boy knew was that a tirradon had been eyeing them from a craggy peak. Just as Aldy fell through the ice the tirradon came swooping down out of nowhere and across the lake, filling the air with its hideous screech and blocking the sky with its monstrous dark body.

"Oh my gosh!" Scotty cried. "NO! NO! NO! What am I gonna do?" Scotty could not catch his breath. He felt like he was going to have a heart attack.

He started talking to himself. "I can't go out there. The tirradon will eat me! I'll fall through the ice, too! I'll freeze! I'll drown! Then I won't be any help to Aldy at all, but I have to help him, but what if I don't, he'll die if I don't help him."

Scotty was panicking, trembling, terrified. He thought, I have to help Aldy, but how? There goes my heart again pounding out of my chest. I'm shaking so badly right now there's no way I could go out on that lake, but I have to, I have to pull Aldy out of the freezing water.

Just then, the tirradon made another pass over the lake and came dangerously close to Aldy this time with its huge sharp talons.

Aldy was struggling so hard to grasp the ice around the hole he had fallen through so that he could pull himself out of the water. "Scotty, help me! I can't grab onto the ice! I'm freezing! Help! Help! Help, meeee-." Aldy's head dipped beneath the water.

Scotty felt sheer terror. He was talking to himself a mile a minute now, "Oh geez, what am I gonna do! W-w-what am I gonna do? Aldy will die if I don't help him. I can't think straight. My mind is racing. Aldy will freeze, he'll die, and we'll never find the Blue Kyrolite. He'll never be king! That tirradon is going to grab him right out of the lake and rip him to shreds, then it will come for me and eat me alive! Oh, no, no, no, I can't stand still, I'm so scared. I don't know what to do."

Time was running out for Aldy. Scotty was pacing back and forth, back and forth at the edge of the lake. Pacing and trembling, trembling and pacing, and praying the tirradon would go away. Scotty thought, if I could only . . . just then Scotty remembered how his mind had become still after he had lost his balance and slid down the witch's wand. Suddenly he stopped dead in his tracks and let go of every thought he had ever had. His mind became so still, so quiet, so peaceful, so calm, and he knew what he had to do.

# CHAPTER 10

# THE BLUE KYROLITE

Scotty stood by the edge of the lake, peaceful and calm. He carefully watched the tirradon as it made another low pass over the lake. His mind was so still he did not even hear the tirradon's hideous screech or notice that it was breathing fire. He kept his eyes on the tirradon's massive spiked tail. As its tail swung past Scotty he wrapped both his arms around one of the spikes, held on tight, and rode the tail of the beast across the lake to where Aldy was desperately trying to pull himself out of the water. As the tirradon made a low pass over the lake Scotty let go of the spike and dropped down on the frozen lake inches from where Aldy had fallen in.

"Aldy, grab my hand! Hold on tight!" Scotty shouted.

While Aldy desperately held on to Scotty's hand, Scotty put his other arm around Aldy's neck and pulled Aldy as hard as he could.

"Aldy grab on to the edge of the ice as soon as you can," Scotty cried.

As Scotty pulled Aldy to the edge of the ice, Aldy grabbed hold of the ice and hoisted himself up out of the icy water that was about to be his grave.

"Let's make a run for the shore!" Scotty shouted over the tirradon's manic shrieks.

"Oh, no, here it comes again!" yelled Aldy.

While the ice cracked underneath their fleeing feet the boys ran as fast as they could across the barely frozen lake. At the same time the screaming, screeching, monstrous beast was making a run for them. With hypersonic speed it dove at them, barely missing them as they fled faster and faster.

They ran and slid and glided, huffing, puffing and shaking from the bitter cold as they made it across the barely frozen lake to the shore, all the while being chased by the screaming devil as it burned holes in the ice with its hot breath and made the lake boil.

"Riff, riff, riff, riff, RIFFFFFFFFFFFF, there, there!" Barty was running in circles, jumping up and down by the edge of the lake and looking off in the distance. As soon as the boys made it to shore Barty grabbed Aldy's frozen, wet hand and led the boys to a little outcropping of rock a few feet from the edge of the lake.

"Good, we can hide here from that monster!" Scotty gasped.

Aldy's drooping antennae were doing wild dances on top of his head. Scotty was worried about his friend.

"Sc-Sc-Scotty," Aldy was trying to catch his breath, "You saved my life. You saved the future king of Kestrellia!"

"I saved my best buddy."

"You're the bravest person I know. No one on Kestrellia would have the nerve to grab hold of a tirradon's tail."

"Me? Brave?"

"Yes, I've always admired your courage. You came all the way from Earth, all by yourself. Space is a cold, dark, lonely place. I have never been in space. You're brave. I bet you were the only kid onboard the transport ship."

"True. There was no one to talk to. I spent most of the time in my room on the ship. I was so happy when we landed, and I saw my dad and Zillian waiting for me at the space port . . . Aldy, enough talk, you're shaking, you're freezing. I'll build a fire. You get some rest."

A very shaken and tired Aldy mumbled, "Scotty, we still, uh, we still have not found the Blue Kyrolite."

"Don't worry we'll-,

Aldy interrupted, "Scotty I am beginning to think that the high priests never really hid anything up here in the mountains."

"We'll find it. I know we will. Now get some rest, future king."

Scotty got to work building a fire with some of the last firesticks the boys had packed. Barty curled up next to Aldy to keep him warm, and Aldy fell asleep. While Scotty warmed himself by the fire he watched his poor, exhausted friend. Aldy's antennae where drooping way down. His orange skin looked faded. He tossed and turned and mumbled, but Scotty could not make out what he was saying.

Suddenly he woke with a jolt saying, "Gems, gems, gems, gems, GEMS!" Aldy's antennae perked up and wriggled and he laughed. "Scotty . . . ha, ha, ha . . . Scotty, I had the strangest, funniest dream. There were gems of all shapes and sizes and shades of blue dancing around my head. They had eyes and big mouths and arms and little hands and they kept poking me with their fingers and saying, 'You'll never find us, you'll never find us, we're hiding right in front of you, but you'll never find us.'"

"And then my father's spiritual teacher, Lorian, came swooping out from nowhere and danced around me singing, 'gems of wisdom, jewels of knowledge, gems of knowledge, jewels of wisdom,' and he was taunting me, too. He kept chanting, 'You can't find them, you can't find them, Aldy, Aldy, you must find them, you can't find them, you can't find them, Aldy, Aldy, YOU MUST FIND THEM!'"

"Talking gems? Lorian? That's crazy!"

"Scotty, I am so confused. Every time my father's spiritual teacher would come to visit he would always talk about gems of knowledge, jewels of wisdom, and tell my father to seek them in order to be a better king."

The boys were quite for awhile, deep in thought about Aldy's strange dream. Scotty shook his head, looked around at the cold, stark mountains, and said,

"Why would a blue gem make you a better king, anyway? Anyone could spot a big, shiny blue gem up here, including Jessup. Aldy, that's it!"

"That's what?"

"Don't you see? Lorian just showed us in your dream what we're really looking for. No wonder we never found a beautiful sparkling blue gem. We're not supposed to be looking for a real gem, we're supposed to be seeking some kind of knowledge, gems of knowledge, jewels of wisdom, that's what he said."

"Scotty you're so smart! You can always see things in ways that I can't. But what knowledge?"

"I don't know. It could be anything."

The boys were too exhausted to figure out this new mystery. They settled back and watched the leaping flames from the fire. Aldy started thinking back to a time when he was very young, when his parents and uncles and grandparents would sit around the table after dinner and talk about the time before he was born.

"Scotty, I'm recalling things I heard years ago when I was a little kid and my family would talk about Jessup's family, especially his great-grandfather.

"My father and I care about our people. Jessup is different. He cares only about himself and what will make him happy. He wants more and more things, houses, space shuttles, riches. He's like a little boy who never grew up. He's just like his great-grandfather. His great-grandfather started a war with the Cerulians hundreds of years ago."

"Why?"

"Because Cerulains had more land than the Larians."

"I see."

"There were awful wars on Kestrellia when Jessup's great-grandfather was king. I remember hearing stories about Larians and Cerulians hurting each other, killing each other, back in what my parents called the 'Dark Days.'"

"Those must have been terrible times."

"Awful, horrible times. Jessup's great-grandfather bombed Cerulian land and destroyed most of the temperate areas."

"Is that why there's so little forest on Kestrellia?"

"Yes, the forests used to stretch for thousands of miles. There were hundreds of species of trees, large lakes and rivers, and birds! Scotty, I remember now, there were birds once on Kestrellia!"

"Well, now I get it. I always wondered why there was so little forest on this planet. The temperate area is–"

Aldy broke in. "–only a hundred miles wide. The forests were destroyed and became wastelands." Aldy took a deep breath. "They're even rumors that Jessup owns laser canons, antimatter disruptors, and other weapons. No one on Kestrellia has weapons anymore. They were outlawed after the Dark Days."

"Why would Jessup have weapons? Do you think he wants the Dark Days to come back? I can't even imagine anything like that. There haven't been any wars on Earth in hundreds of years. Grownups almost destroyed the planet and every person on it centuries ago. That's when the human race realized they had to find a way to live in peace."

"Yes, just like we Kestrellians did after the Dark Days. I can really, clearly see now that Jessup is just like his great-grandfather. He *is* evil. He does not care about Kestrellians or the planet. Jessup is ten years older than I am, but he has not become a grownup, and he never will. He'll never understand that wealth, possessions, control, and power are not important."

The boys were quite for a moment, thinking about how nasty Jessup was and imaging a Kestrellia where Jessup was king. Finally, Scotty said, "I think you've got it! I think you found the real Blue Kyrolite."

"I do get *it*! I do! That is it, Scotty! That *is* the great jewel we have been searching for! I know what it will take to be a good king now. Wealth and power mean nothing! When I'm a grownup I must do everything I can to make my people happy and take care of the planet. No wars ever again! Just peace and caring for each other and the planet, maybe we could even find a way to reclaim the wastelands. Hey, maybe the birds will come back to Kestrellia someday."

"Aldy, my friend, I think you've found the most beautiful, precious jewel of all. You'll make an awesome king!" Scotty declared.

Aldy smiled a smile Scotty had not seen in long time and his antennae perked up and danced in circles.

"I think our quest for the Blue Kyrolite is over. Let's head back down the mountain in the morning to our families and those hot sunny wastelands with our new friend Barty. I think we've both had enough of these cold, creepy mountains."

That night the boys and Barty slept like babies.

## CHAPTER 11

# THE HOMECOMING

The boys woke early the next day. They had to skip breakfast since there was no food left. They packed quickly and practically ran down the trail through the mountains to the lowlands.

"I can't wait to get back!"

"Me, either."

As they came out through the mountains, Scotty was running ahead of Aldy and Barty, and as he headed down the part of the trail that was bounded on one side by the drop off to the deep valley, Aldy yelled, "Scotty, be careful, you might slip off the edge."

"Hey, no problem, gravity will keep me on the trail!"

When the boys arrived at Aldy's house they were greeted by the high priests, Aldy's whole family, Zillian, and Scotty's very worried father. The boys had been gone longer than they realized. Just as they suspected, they had lost track of time high up in the cold wilderness.

"Well," said Aldy's father, "where is the Blue Kyrolite that you went to find?"

The high priests immediately encircled Aldy as he pointed to his head and heart and said, "I found something in my head and heart that is much more valuable, much more important, and much more beautiful than a sparkling blue gem. I now know what it really means to be king. I know what kind of grownup I must become. I know that wealth and power are unimportant. The happiness of my people and their wellbeing and the welfare of the planet are what will guide my life when I am a grownup king."

Aldy's father and the high priests smiled.

"You found the most precious gem in the world, my son."

In their deep voices the high priests said in unison, "You have succeeded in the quest. You will make a fine king someday."

Then Aldy added, "And I'm not the only one who learned something amazing up in the mountains. Scotty was on a quest, too."

"Me? A quest? For what?"

"Yes, Scotty, you stilled your mind and found peace, bravery, and confidence. In fact, you're one of the bravest souls in the universe."

Scotty's cheeks became red and hot, but this time not because he was afraid of something, this time it was because he was embarrassed and blushing.

Then Aldy announced, "Scotty saved my life!"

"What?" Scotty's father cried out in sheer and utter disbelief.

"What?" echoed Zillian.

"What?" said the king.

"WHAAAAATTTTTT?" boomed the high priests with their deep voices and strange accents.

"Dad, remember the lake high up in the mountains where we used to camp when I was a kid? Well, it's frozen, partially frozen, that is. I foolishly went running out onto the lake and fell through the ice and Scotty grabbed a tirradon's tail–"

"A tirradon's tail?" the shocked king interrupted.

". . . and he used its tail to get across the lake to where I was struggling to get out of the icy water. And Scotty pulled me out and helped me run across the lake to safety."

"Scotty, you did *what?*" his dad asked still in sheer disbelief.

"I did, but first I stilled my mind. My mind became very silent and peaceful. I let go of all my crazy thoughts, and I knew that there was nothing in this universe to be afraid of and that I could do anything. Then I grabbed a spike on the tirradon's tail, and . . ."

His dad could not contain himself and blurted out, "Amazing! I'm so proud of you, son!"

The king bowed to Scotty and said, "Thank you for saving my son's life."

Now the high priests surrounded Scotty, and boomed in their deep voices with their strange accents,

"You are a brave soul, young Scotty, all of Krestrellia will thank you someday. You saved the life of the boy who will be their king. They will sing your praises. Poems and books will be written about you."

"I saved my best friend. That's all I did."

Aldy said, "What a summer vacation this has turned out to be for you . . ."

". . . and there's still a few weeks left of it. And the very best part of all is that I'll be back next summer!"